QB BLITZ

MATT CHRISTOPHER®

QB BLITZ

LITTLE, BROWN AND COMPANY
NEW YORK • BOSTON

Little, Brown and Company

Hachette Book Group
237 Park Avenue, New York, NY 10017
Visit our website at www.lb-kids.com

www.mattchristopher.com

Little, Brown and Company is a division of Hachette Book Group, Inc.
The Little, Brown name and logo are trademarks of
Hachette Book Group, Inc.

The publisher is not responsible for websites (or their content) that are not
owned by the publisher.

First Edition: September 2011

The characters and events portrayed in this book are fictitious.
Any similarity to real persons, living or dead, is coincidental and
not intended by the author.

Matt Christopher® is a registered trademark of
Matt Christopher Royalties, Inc.

Text written by Stephanie True Peters

Library of Congress Cataloging-in-Publication Data

Peters, Stephanie True, 1965–
QB blitz / text by Stephanie Peters. — 1st ed.
p. cm.—(Matt Christopher the #1 sports series for kids)
Summary: Cal became a hero as the only seventh grader on his middle school
football team, but now his former teammates are in high school and a popular
new player is challenging him for the quarterback position by turning the coach
and other players against Cal.
ISBN 978-0-316-17682-8
[1. Football—Fiction. 2. Competition (Psychology)—Fiction. 3. Popularity—
Fiction. 4. Middle schools—Fiction. 5. Schools—Fiction.] I. Title.
PZ7.P441833Qb 2011
[Fic]—dc22

2011002280

10 9 8 7 6 5 4 3 2 1

CW

Printed in the United States of America

QB BLITZ

1

Break!"

Cal Kelliher and his teammates applauded madly as quarterback Charlie Nielsen and the Hurricanes offense moved from the huddle to the line of scrimmage. Cal cupped his hands around his mouth and bellowed, "C'mon, Charlie, make it happen!"

It was a Monday afternoon in late November, and the Hurricanes were facing the Chargers for the last game of the season. Excitement and tension filled the air, for both teams had undefeated records. The Hurricanes had led at the end of the first half, but the Chargers had overtaken them in the third quarter. Now, with less than a minute remaining in the final period, the score was Chargers 16, Hurricanes 12. If the Hurricanes were to go home with the win, they needed a touchdown.

That touchdown was just within reach. The Hurricanes had the ball at the Chargers 22-yard line. It was first-and-ten. Charlie had been playing like a champ all day. Most of the gains had been from run plays, but Charlie also had a rocket for an arm. If he could complete one long pass—

"Hut one! Hut two! Hike!"

DeShawn Rodgers, the Hurricanes center, snapped the ball to Charlie. But as Charlie faded back, DeShawn suddenly lost his footing in the churned-up turf. He fell, leaving a wide-open gap.

The Charger nose tackle sprang through the hole and made straight for Charlie. Charlie saw him coming but not soon enough to get rid of the ball—or to get out of the way, either.

Wham! The Hurricanes quarterback was completely leveled by a bone-crushing assault for a loss of five yards. The nose tackle leaped to his feet, whooping and punching the sky in victory as his teammates surrounded him.

Cal's heart sank as he watched the Chargers celebrate. As the Hurricanes backup quarterback, he knew how demoralizing it could be to get sacked.

I wonder how Charlie's handling it. Cal glanced at Charlie and froze. The quarterback was writhing on the ground, gripping his knee.

"Coach!" Cal yelled.

But Coach Fredericks and the Hurricanes trainer were already rushing onto the field. They crouched over the fallen player. Minutes passed. Then, at last, the two men helped Charlie up. Fans and members of both teams applauded as the injured quarterback was half carried to the sidelines.

When Charlie was safely on the bench with an ice pack on his knee, Coach Fredericks beckoned to Cal. "You're going in for Charlie," he said.

Cal gulped down his sudden nervousness. "Do I have time for a few warm-up throws?"

"You won't need any for what you're going to do," the coach replied. "Now listen closely, because this is a once-in-a-lifetime play." Then he outlined what he wanted Cal to do.

Cal's eyes widened. "Is—is that even legal?" he asked. "I mean, if I make it into the end zone, will the touchdown stand?"

The coach gave a sly grin. "It will. But the play's success depends on you. If you time it right and really sell it, it should work like a dream. If not"—he jerked his chin at the Chargers defense milling around on the field—"be prepared to end up at the bottom of a pig pile."

Cal gulped again.

"One last thing, Cal," Coach Fredericks said. "Don't tell our guys what you're planning. If they know, they might give it away."

Cal nodded. "You can count on me, Coach." His voice came out strong and assured, but as he ran onto the field, his insides were quaking.

The other Hurricanes gathered for the huddle. Cal, the only seventh grader, suddenly felt very small compared with the taller, brawnier eighth graders. He felt smaller still when they all looked at him as if he were crazy when he told them he wasn't allowed to reveal the play.

"What?" DeShawn said.

"You're supposed to line up so I'm protected," Cal said. "Then follow my lead."

"Follow your lead?" DeShawn repeated incredulously. "What the heck does that mean?"

"Trust me," Cal pleaded. "It's what Coach Fredericks told me to do."

DeShawn didn't look pleased, but he knew better than to question the coach's instructions. "Okay, you heard him," he said to his teammates. "Let's go."

The line of scrimmage was now at the Chargers 27-yard line. The Hurricanes clustered close to the middle, and the Chargers took their positions opposite them.

Cal took a deep breath. *Here goes nothing,* he thought. Then he called the play.

DeShawn shoved the ball into Cal's hands. At that exact moment, Cal straightened and looked at the ball as if something were wrong with it.

"Hold on, hold on, wait a second!" he said in his most bewildered voice. Then he started walking toward the sidelines, still holding the ball.

Perplexed, all the players on the field, Hurricanes and Chargers alike, stood up.

Coach Fredericks took a step toward Cal. "Is something wrong with the ball?" His

6

brow was furrowed, but Cal was close enough to see that his eyes were twinkling with glee.

Behind him, he heard players from both teams murmuring in growing confusion. And then—

"Go!" hissed the coach.

Cal spun on his heel, tucked the football under his arm, and began to race for the end zone.

"What the—?" The closest Charger jumped back in astonishment. "What're you doing?"

Cal ignored him and kept running.

"Hey!" the Charger yelled to his teammates. "I think—I think he's trying to score! Get him!"

The Charger was right. The ball was in play because Cal had taken the hike. He hadn't called timeout. It wasn't his fault if the defense hadn't tackled him!

Haven't tackled me yet, he amended, for

now that the cat was out of the bag, he could hear the defense pounding after him. He willed himself to run faster than he had ever run before.

"Kelliher is at the twenty!" he heard the announcer cry. "Now he's at the fifteen! But here come the Chargers, and boy, do they look mad!"

With one last burst of speed, Cal crossed the 10-yard line, the five, and then, a split second before an infuriated Charger grabbed him, he lunged into the end zone, ball stretched out in front of him.

"Ooof!" The air whooshed from his lungs when he hit the ground. The Charger leaped over him, catching him in the ribs. Cal grimaced in pain but didn't move. He was waiting to hear the referee's call. It came a moment later.

"Touchdown!"

2

Cal's game-winning trick play was the talk of the middle school the next week. When a Hurricanes fan posted her video of the play on the Internet, Cal became an overnight sensation. The local news even showed the clip at the end of its sports roundup.

"Thanks to Cal Kelliher, the Hurricanes' undefeated season was saved," the announcer said with a wide smile. "Our congratulations go out to him and his teammates."

Cal was a little embarrassed by all the sudden attention—and more than a little worried that Charlie Nielsen would be angry. After all, Charlie was the main reason the Hurricanes had entered that final game undefeated.

He was also the reason Cal had improved as a quarterback that season. From almost the first practice, Charlie had taken Cal under his wing, going over the plays and discussing the finer points of throwing, handing off, taking the snap, and more.

"Why are you bothering to help me so much?" Cal had wondered at one point.

"Simple: The team will be stronger with two good quarterbacks," Charlie had answered.

Still, Cal was relieved when Charlie took his new celebrity in stride. In fact, Charlie continued to go out of his way to be Cal's friend. He invited Cal to sit with him and the other eighth graders at lunch. When they both made the middle school basketball team, Charlie, who was working with his newly healed knee, helped Cal improve his skills by playing one-on-one with him most weekends. He encouraged Cal to try out for spring soccer after basketball ended even though Cal had never played the sport except during gym class. Cal was stunned when he made the team, and although he spent most of the games sitting on the bench, he didn't care. Charlie was one of the most popular eighth graders at the school. When Cal was with him, Charlie's friends treated Cal as a friend, too, even though he was only in seventh grade.

The school year ended in the middle of June with a big send-off for the graduating eighth graders. After the celebration, Cal gave Charlie a gift certificate to the local pizza place, along with a card that read *Congratulations, Graduate!*

"Thanks, man," Charlie said as he slipped the certificate into his wallet and glanced at the card. "We'll have to get together this summer and share a pie."

Cal stuck his hands deep into his pockets. "I can't," he said. "My family and I are heading to our summer place on the lake first thing tomorrow morning. We won't be back until the week before school starts."

"Summer on a lake, huh? Sounds like fun."

"It usually is," Cal admitted. He brightened. "Hey, maybe you could come for a visit sometime! My dad goes back and forth between our house here and our summer place pretty often. He could bring you, no problem. Here, I'll write the phone number on the card."

Charlie handed him the graduation card. "I'll take the number, but I doubt I'll make it up. July is looking pretty busy for me, what with overnight camps and stuff. And August is going to be all about getting ready for freshman football, so…" His voice drifted off, and he shrugged.

"Oh, sure, of course," Cal said, fishing

12

around in his backpack for a pen. "Well, you'll have the number if you change your—"

"Hey, DeShawn, wait up!" Charlie suddenly yelled. "Sorry, Cal, I gotta go. DeShawn's supposed to be giving me a ride to the eighth-grade pool party. I'd invite you along, but it's just for eighth graders, you know? So see you, and have a great summer on that lake!"

With that, Charlie took off to catch up with DeShawn, leaving Cal holding the card and the pen he'd finally found. Cal started to call after him, but then he closed his mouth. He'd feel terrible if Charlie missed his ride. Besides, he could always e-mail him the phone number.

Cal, his two sisters, and his parents left for the lake before dawn the next morning. Cal rode with his father in one car, while his mother took the girls. They all arrived at noon and spent the rest of the day unpacking and setting up the house. After every room was cleaned, Mrs. Kelliher and the girls headed to the grocery store while Cal and Mr. Kelliher went to the community boathouse to get their kayaks and canoes out of storage. Then they all made the rounds to the other lake houses to see which of their summer friends were back.

It was because of those friends that Cal and his sisters found it bearable to be away from their hometown all summer. For more than ten years, the Kellihers and seven other families had shared the lake and one another's company. They spent the warm-weather weeks swimming, boating, camping out, playing games, and taking turns hosting barbecues and bonfires. There was never a lack of things to do, even when it rained.

Cal had always loved every minute of his time on the lake, and this summer would have been perfect, too, except for one thing: Charlie never got in touch with him. Cal had e-mailed him the house's number, but after a few weeks of grabbing the phone every time it rang, Cal accepted that Charlie probably wouldn't be calling. He was disappointed, but he reasoned that his friend had warned that he would have a busy summer. So Cal put Charlie and everything else about his hometown out of his mind.

Then one night in mid-August, the air turned so cool that Cal was forced to use an extra blanket. He lay on his stomach in bed, listening to an owl hooting and thinking about school and the upcoming football season.

I wonder if the Hurricanes will be as good as we were last year. Probably not, since Charlie and the other starters are in high school now. He rolled over and laced his fingers behind his head. *Of course, that means that their slots are up for grabs. And since no one else played quarterback last year...*

He grinned at the ceiling. *I can hear it now: At quarterback for the Hurricanes, Ca-a-al Kelliher! Yeah. I like the sound of that!*

3

One week later, Cal and his family closed up their lake house, said good-bye to their summer friends, and headed for home. Cal was unpacking his suitcase when his older sister, Tracy, knocked on his door.

"Mail call!" She tossed a thick envelope onto his bed and left.

The letter was from the middle school athletics department. Inside was the usual permission form, a request for an up-to-date physical signed by his doctor, and a practice and game schedule.

On top of the other papers was a form letter addressed to all returning Hurricanes players.

Cal assumed it was from Coach Fredericks until he glanced at the signature. It was from the middle school football coach, all right, but the last name was Jennings, not Fredericks. Confused, Cal sat on his bed to read it.

Dear Player:

As you may already know, Mr. Fredericks has accepted a new position as principal of Mountain Middle School in Greenview. Mr. Fredericks had hoped to continue as the Hurricanes coach this year, but his new responsibilities prevent him from doing so. Therefore, I will be stepping in as your new coach. I look forward to seeing you all at our preseason meeting this Saturday at one o'clock and to continuing the success of the Hurricanes football program.

Sincerely,
Samuel Jennings

Cal stared at the name for a long moment. Then he went to his bookshelf and pulled out his seventh-grade yearbook. In the teachers section, he found the picture he was looking for: Samuel Jennings, music department. Seeing it made Cal believe it.

He groaned. He had taken music with Mr. Jennings in both sixth and seventh grade. Of all his "specials"—gym, theater, art, shop—music was his least favorite. It wasn't that he didn't like music; he just preferred to listen to it rather than learn about it or, worse, perform it. He still cringed whenever he remembered the time in sixth grade when he'd played a made-up tune on an instrument he'd crafted from recycled items. He had no ear for music and knew his song sounded terrible, but that didn't prepare him for the laughter that came when he'd finished. Even Mr. Jennings had worn a smile.

Ever since then, Cal had dreaded his

class with Mr. Jennings. And now he'd be seeing him every afternoon for the whole fall!

The next day, Mrs. Kelliher dropped Cal off at the middle school for the football meeting. Cal started toward the front door when he noticed the freshman football team taking a water break at the field next to the school. He was early for the meeting, so he hurried over to say hello to his old friends.

"Hey, DeShawn, long time no see!" Cal called to the first boy he saw. "How's it going? Did you have a good summer?"

The burly center looked up and gave Cal a quick nod. Then he started talking to one of the other players.

Cal spotted Charlie next. He grinned broadly and waved to catch the quarterback's attention. Charlie smiled and waved back. He looked as if he was about to come over when a man with a whistle and a clip-board called his name. Moments later, the two were deep in conversation. After waiting a minute or two, Cal realized he had to leave or be late for his meeting.

"DeShawn, do me a favor and tell Charlie to give me a call, okay?" he said.

"Oh, yeah, I'll be sure to do that," DeShawn replied.

"Thanks, man!" It was only after Cal had taken a few steps that he registered the sarcasm in DeShawn's voice. He glanced over his shoulder in time to see the center roll his eyes as his teammates burst out laughing.

Stung, Cal turned back and speed-walked into the middle school. Other boys were going in, too, clearly on their way to the meeting. A few of them greeted Cal, but his face was still burning from embarrassment, so he ducked his head and simply muttered "hey" in reply. Inside the gym, he took a seat high up in the bleachers and sank down, willing his color to return to normal.

A minute later, the door to the boys' locker room opened, and Mr. Jennings and two beefy young men filed into the gym. Mr. Jennings stood in front of the team, patiently waiting for the noise to die down. Then he introduced the two other men as Lukas and Owen, his assistant coaches. He explained that they were graduate students from the nearby university.

"They're former football players, too," Mr. Jennings added.

After the introductions, Mr. Jennings began explaining his expectations for the coming season. It was the standard speech about sportsmanship, teamwork, regular attendance, and the players' roles as representatives of their school and community.

Cal had heard the same sort of lecture before, so he tuned it out and let his gaze wander over the other players. He recognized several, including Fred Hawkins, who had played wide receiver and safety last year; center Will Bishop, who had doubled as a defensive lineman; and Mario and Raul Torrez, identical twins who were running backs on offense and linebackers on defense. Like Cal, they were all eighth graders now; like him, they had spent the previous season coming off the bench. He supposed they were just as hopeful as he was of earning a starting slot.

Then he saw a blond-haired boy he didn't recognize staring at him. Their eyes met for a brief second, and then the boy dropped his gaze.

I wonder who that is, Cal thought. He soon found out.

Mr. Jennings had finished his speech and was moving on to the next order of business. "When I call out a position, I want everyone who is interested in playing it to stand up. Quarterback?"

Cal got to his feet. So did the blond boy. Everyone else stayed seated.

"Guess it's just you and me," the boy said. He turned to Mr. Jennings. "I'm Jordan Stahl. I'm starting seventh grade here this year, but some of you might not know me, because I didn't live here until this summer."

"Aw, c'mon, J-Bird. Everybody knows you!" Fred said, playfully punching Jordan in the leg.

Jordan cut a look at Cal. "Well, not *everybody*." Then he sat down.

Cal was wondering why Jordan seemed instantly popular when Coach Owen pointed at him. "I know you. You're Cal Kelliher, the kid who did that trick play against the Chargers last year, right?"

Cal jammed his hands in his pockets and tried to look modest. "Yeah, that's me. You've seen the video, huh?"

To Cal's surprise, the assistant coach

glared at him. "Oh, I've seen it, all right. Remember that first Charger you ran past? That's my little brother. Thanks to you, he was the laughingstock of his school. He was so humiliated that he refused to go out for the team this year."

"Oh." At a loss for words, Cal sank back down to his seat. When Mr. Jennings asked him to confirm that he wanted to play quarterback again this year, he just nodded.

It took fifteen more minutes for Mr. Jennings to meet the rest of the players. When he was done, he told the boys they could leave after they'd picked out their jerseys. Cal wanted to push to the front to get his favorite number, eleven, but he hung back instead, feeling awkward after Coach Owen's outburst. Then he saw Jordan holding up the shirt with the double ones on it.

"Hey, Jordan, that's my shirt," Cal said, clattering down the bleacher steps. "I mean,

I've worn that number for the past two seasons, and I'd like to wear it again."

Jordan looked from Cal to the shirt and back again. "It's too small for you."

Cal frowned. "No, it isn't! C'mon, man, there are lots of other numbers to choose from." He reached out to grab the jersey.

Jordan pulled it back. "I'm telling you, you're not going to fit in it!"

Mr. Jennings appeared. "Is there a problem?"

Jordan's expression turned innocent. "No, sir. I was just handing this to Cal." He tossed the jersey to Cal.

"Thanks," Cal muttered. He turned to go.

"Why don't you model it for us?" Jordan said suddenly.

"Yeah, try it on, Cal," other boys chimed in.

With a shrug, Cal tugged the shirt over his head. It wasn't even halfway down his torso when he realized that Jordan was right. Once he put on his pads, the jersey wasn't going to fit. Embarrassed, he pulled it off, threw it at Jordan, and grabbed a different shirt from the bin of extra-larges. Then he spun on his heel and banged out the door.

4

*B*llllarrrrr!

Cal rolled over, shut off his alarm clock, and sighed. It was Monday morning, the first day of school. He hadn't been up so early since the last day of seventh grade and was grateful to find an empty seat on the bus. He slumped next to the window, staring out at the passing houses without really seeing them.

Cal perked up once he got to school. He was surprised to see how much his class-mates had changed over the summer; there were some he hardly recognized. He guessed he must have looked different, too, since some kids returned his wave of greeting as if they weren't sure who he was.

It wasn't until lunchtime that it dawned on him that maybe they knew who he was—but weren't sure they wanted to wave back.

Cal hadn't eaten much breakfast, so he was starving when he entered the cafeteria. By force of habit, he made his way toward the table by the corner window. Last year, that table was "owned" by the eighth-grade football players, but after the trick-play game, Cal had been allowed to sit there, too.

Cal grinned when he saw that once again, eighth-grade football players filled the corner table's seats. Then he saw Jordan Stahl sitting there. His smile faded.

He shouldn't be there! He's in seventh grade!

The moment the thought entered his head, Cal knew it was childish. None of the eighth graders had cared when he'd sat there last year. In fact, they'd welcomed him.

Hadn't they?

An image of DeShawn rolling his eyes flashed across Cal's brain. Suddenly, he wasn't so sure how welcome he'd really been.

Laughter from the football table broke into his thoughts. Jordan was standing up and pantomiming putting on a shirt. With a jolt, Cal realized that he was watching an exaggerated replay of the jersey incident from Saturday's meeting.

In that same instant, Jordan glanced up and saw him. But rather than stop his comedy routine, he became even more animated, tossing the imaginary jersey aside with a flourish. "I need an XXL," he said in a snobby tone. "Anything smaller won't fit—over my swelled head, that is!" He finished by posing like the Heisman Trophy.

Again, the table of football players burst into laughter. "Good one, man!" Fred Hawkins cried.

Jordan gave Fred a grin and started to sit down. As he did, he looked back at Cal—and froze as if he'd just noticed him. When he spoke, his voice was full of contrition.

"Oh, um, hi, Cal. I didn't see you there. But, uh, I guess you saw me." He held his hands up as if to halt Cal in his tracks, though Cal hadn't taken a step. "Listen, I'm sorry, man, okay? It was just a little humor. Come join us. Guys, make room—and stop laughing, will you?"

If Cal hadn't known any better, he would have said Jordan was genuinely embarrassed about having been caught mocking him. He might have even accepted the apology and the invitation to sit. But he did know better, just as he knew that Jordan was still laughing at him now. So instead, he turned and started walking away.

"Oh, man, I really blew it," he heard Jordan say. "You think I should go talk to him?"

"Aw, don't sweat it," Fred replied. "It's not your fault he can't take a joke."

"Well, if you're sure," Jordan said.

Cal was too far away to hear if Fred had anything more to say. He sat at an empty table and opened his lunch bag. A sandwich, chips, and cookies disappeared into his mouth. But he didn't taste a bite of his food.

"Okay, boys, we have only an hour and a half for practice," Mr. Jennings announced. "Warm up so we can get down to business."

Cal and the rest of the Hurricanes were gathered on the football field. The day had turned hot, and by the end of the calisthenics, Cal was sweating. Mr. Jennings insisted they drink plenty of water—"I don't want anyone passing out because of dehydration!"—and then instructed the assistant coaches to take everyone but Cal; Jordan; and wide receivers Fred Hawkins, Juan Morales, and Ronnie Anderson to the far end of the field.

"We'll start with an easy passing drill," Mr. Jennings said to his group. He paired Cal with Fred and Jordan with Juan, stationing the two quarterbacks at the 10-yard line and the wide receivers across from them at the fifteen. He told Ronnie to pay attention because he'd have a turn soon. Then he tossed footballs to Cal and Jordan and told them to get down on their throwing-arm knees.

"This exercise will loosen up your shoulders and help you improve your accuracy," Mr. Jennings said when the boys were in position. "Go through your throwing motions so I can take a look at your mechanics. Cal, you first."

Cal gripped the football with his right

hand. His pinkie and ring fingers were touching the laces, and his middle and pointer fingers were on either side of the ball's back stripe. His thumb was on the far side, forming a U-shape with his pointer. At Mr. Jennings's command, he raised the ball straight over his shoulder, palm facing out and thumb down, and twisted at the waist so his throwing arm was back and his other shoulder was forward. Then, in one fluid movement, he twisted back around and threw, rotating his hand so that his fingers spun the ball in a spiral as he released it. Even though the throw didn't have much power, the ball traveled far enough to reach Fred.

Mr. Jennings nodded approvingly and then told Jordan to do the same thing.

Jordan started to move the ball into throwing position, but he suddenly stopped and studied his grip. He smiled as if making a delightful discovery. "You know, I never noticed this before, but the way I hold the football is sort of like the way I hold my trumpet, except I'm using my little finger, too."

"You play the trumpet?" Mr. Jennings asked.

"I was going to play in the jazz band at my old school this year," Jordan answered. "But then we moved." He lifted and lowered a shoulder.

"You know I put together a jazz band at this school, don't you?" Mr. Jennings said. "Tryouts are in two weeks. If you're interested, come by my office, and I'll give you the music to prepare for the audition."

"Really? Awesome!" Jordan sounded excited, but in the next second that excitement faded. "I'm only in seventh grade, though. Do many younger kids make it into the band?"

"I judge by ability, not by age," Mr.

Jennings informed him. "And that goes for out here, too."

"Good to know," Jordan said. Then he launched a beautiful spiral pass that hit Juan right in the hands.

5

Cal and Jordan continued to work with the receivers and Mr. Jennings for the rest of practice. They moved from the bent-knee drill to throwing from a standing position with their hips squared toward their partners and their feet firmly planted. They started ten yards apart but gradually increased the distance between them. Cal was paired with Fred for ten passes, and then Ronnie took Fred's place, Fred switched into Juan's spot, and Juan took a quick break.

Ronnie was shorter than Fred, but Cal had no trouble adjusting his throw to his new target. Jordan, on the other hand, needed several tries before he hit Fred in the hands.

"That's it, J-Bird! Now you got it!" Fred called after three successful catches.

Mr. Jennings changed the drill again. First, he had Cal and Jordan stand with their right feet forward, toes pointing in the direction of the throw. "This will feel awkward," he told them, "because as right-handers, your natural throwing motion is with the left foot in front. But you won't always be in that position, so it's important to get used to throwing wrong-footed. Instead of thinking about how it feels, focus on your targets and getting your hips into the motion every time."

They each launched twenty passes and then switched their feet and threw twenty from their normal stances. Cal had a few misfires, but for the most part he found the receivers with the ball.

Jordan, on the other hand, seemed to have difficulty adjusting to each new drill. Mr. Jennings had to stop and walk him through the motions before Jordan got the hang of it.

Cal was feeling secretly pleased with his own superior performance—until he overheard Jordan say, "You're a really good coach, Mr. Jennings. You explain what I'm doing wrong, tell me how to change it, and when I do, everything clicks into place." He shook his head as if amazed. "Honestly, after your help, I feel like I've been throwing the right way forever!"

Mr. Jennings laughed. "Well, helping players improve *is* what I'm here for, after all."

Jordan nodded enthusiastically. "And I know I speak for Cal and everyone else when I say we're lucky to have you. Right, Cal?"

Cal mumbled his agreement yet couldn't

help thinking that the coach would have to be thick in the skull not to know Jordan was kissing up to him. But Mr. Jennings simply accepted the compliment with an incline of his head.

Mr. Jennings put the quarterbacks and receivers through two more drills. The first had the pairs running parallel down the lines with Cal passing to Juan and Jordan to Ronnie while in motion. In the second, Jordan, Fred, Juan, and Ronnie formed a wide circle around Cal, who had the ball.

"Stand still while they move around you," Mr. Jennings said to Cal. "I'll call out 'freeze' and then a name. As quickly as you can, find that person and throw to him. Concentrate on everything we've been working on this afternoon: accuracy, power, proper mechanics, and so forth. Ready?"

At Cal's nod, the four players began to circle him in a counterclockwise direction. Cal held the football in both hands chest high, ready to fire off the pass.

"Freeze!" the coach shouted. "Juan!"

Cal's brain quickly registered Jordan and Fred standing in front of him and Ronnie to his left. So he spun to his right, lifting the ball for the throw as he turned. His instincts had been correct; that's where Juan was. Cal launched the pass. Juan caught it without having to move a step. Grinning, he tossed the ball back to Cal, who readied himself for the next throw.

Again, the circle of four started moving around him. Cal tensed, waiting for the call. This time, it was Fred's name that was uttered.

Zip! The ball spiraled on a line from Cal to Fred. Fred returned it with an easy toss. The drill continued this way for a while. Then the coach changed the exercise so that the four were allowed to move in either direction around the circle.

Cal did his best to keep track of their locations, but it wasn't easy with them shifting every which way and passing one another now and then.

"Freeze!" Mr. Jennings cried. "Ronnie!"

Ronnie had just moved past Jordan when his name was called. He halted his stride and waited. Cal rifled off his pass. But as the ball left his hands, Jordan suddenly lunged forward and batted it to the ground.

"Hey! What did you do that for?" Cal demanded.

Jordan blinked several times as if surprised by Cal's outburst. Then he gave the coach an appealing look. "This drill is supposed to help us work on getting the ball to the open receiver." He pointed to the ball on the turf. "Ronnie wasn't open. So Cal shouldn't have passed to him."

Mr. Jennings rubbed his chin. "That's not part of the drill as I outlined it, but you've got a point." He turned to Cal. "From now on, only throw the pass if your man is free. If he's covered, hold on to the ball. But," he added, sweeping his eyes over the others, "I don't want any of you reaching for the ball. If you can block it easily, do so. Otherwise, let the receiver make the catch."

Cal retrieved the ball. He went through the exercise several more times. Then he stepped into the circle so Jordan could have a turn. Cal looked for the chance to bat one of Jordan's passes down, but that chance never came. Still, he noted with satisfaction, Jordan seemed so concerned with passing quickly rather than accurately that oftentimes his targets had to shift to catch the ball.

Jordan's turn ended when the practice ended. On the sidelines, Cal was sure he saw the first genuine emotion of the afternoon cross Jordan's face. That emotion was pure frustration.

In the locker room, however, Jordan

appeared more embarrassed than frus-
trated.

"Boy, was I ever lousy out there! I mean,
phew! Talk about stinking up the joint!"

"Aw, you weren't that bad," Juan reas-
sured him.

"Are you *kidding?*" Jordan gave a short
bark of laughter. "Half my passes were off!"

"Give yourself a break, man," Fred said.
"Everyone makes mistakes."

"Yeah, but as many as I just made?"
Jordan's voice dropped, as if he just realized
himself how bad he had truly been. "Cal
didn't make anywhere near as many."

Cal had been changing behind a nearby
row of lockers. He hadn't meant to eaves-
drop, but when he heard his name, he froze
so he could listen.

"Can I tell you guys something?" Jordan
said. "I think I messed up in that last drill
because Cal made me nervous. You both
heard how he'd yelled at me out there,

right? And today at lunch, he looked like he wanted to strangle me. Saturday, too, when I accidentally took his jersey. Has he always been that mean?"

Cal's jaw dropped. Jordan, a kid he barely knew, had practically called him a bully!

6

Cal shoved his gear into his duffel bag as quickly as possible, hoping to escape the locker room before Jordan or the other boys realized he'd been listening. But just as he reached the door, Mr. Jennings called his name.

"I'd like to see you and Jordan before you go," he said.

Now what? Cal thought as he took a seat in Mr. Jennings's office. Jordan joined them. The coach handed the younger boy a spiral binder.

"This is a copy of last year's playbook," Mr. Jennings told Jordan. "Cal, I believe you have one already?"

In reply, Cal pulled a similar binder out of his duffel bag. Coach Fredericks had given it to him the previous season with instructions to memorize it cover to cover.

Eager to prove himself, Cal had done just that and more. In addition to learning the plays, he'd studied the receivers and running backs. In the margins of the playbook, he'd jotted down his impressions of the players' strengths and weaknesses alongside plays they were involved in.

Next to a pass play, for example, he'd written that Fred tended to look over his shoulder for the ball long before the throw was likely to come. In Cal's opinion, that habit alerted the defense that he was the intended receiver. Two days later, Coach Fredericks warned Fred about that very tendency. Hearing his own thoughts echoed by the coach gave Cal a boost of confidence.

But now Coach Fredericks was gone. Mr. Jennings had already made it clear he would choose the player with the best ability for the quarterback job. But just what he considered "best," Cal had no idea.

As if he'd read Cal's mind, Mr. Jennings now said, "I'm not sure how Coach Fredericks did things, but when it comes to selecting a quarterback to start a game, I look for equal parts ability, attitude, and effort. One way you can prove your willingness to work hard is to memorize these plays. Take the next week to learn what's in these pages, and then I'll collect the binders from you. Any questions?"

Cal shifted uncomfortably. "I'm sorry, but why do I have to turn my binder in? I'm asking only because when Coach Fredericks gave it to me, I thought it was mine to keep," he added hurriedly.

Mr. Jennings pressed his fingertips together. "It is yours, Cal, and I promise you'll get it back when the season is over. But as I said, I expect you to have the plays memorized. If you have the binder, you may be tempted to use it as a crutch. Understood?"

Cal opened his mouth to protest further, but then he caught the look Mr. Jennings was giving him. So instead he just muttered "gotcha" and stood up to leave.

Jordan stayed seated. "Is there anything else, sir? Or may I be dismissed?"

Cal glanced at Mr. Jennings, who was regarding him coolly. "Sorry, I—I just assumed we were through," he said, starting to sit back down.

"We are," Mr. Jennings replied. "You may go."

Face flaming, Cal rose from his half crouch, grabbed his duffel, and hurried out of the locker room with the binder tucked under his arm. A few players were still waiting by the parking lot for their parents to pick them up. Cal nodded to them but didn't say anything.

The locker room door banged open, and Jordan emerged. Cal expected him to join the others, but to his surprise Jordan sidled up to him, open playbook in hand.

"So we've got twelve plays to learn," Jordan said as he thumbed through the pages. "Think you'll be able to memorize them in a week?"

Cal shrugged. "Actually, there are fourteen. And I know them already."

"Do you really? Wow, that's impressive." Jordan eyed Cal's binder. "Wait a minute, did you say fourteen? I have only twelve. Can I see which ones I'm missing?"

Before Cal could react, Jordan had snatched the binder out from under his arm and opened it.

"Hey!" Cal cried. "Give me that!" He tried to grab the binder back, but Jordan, his eyes moving rapidly over the page before him, moved just out of reach.

Cal's shout drew the attention of the other players. "What's going on?" Will Bishop asked.

"He took my playbook," Cal fumed.

Will frowned. "Why would he do that?"

Jordan shut the binder with a snap and thrust it back to Cal. "I'm sorry! Here!" he said, his eyes wide. He turned to the others. "Coach just gave me the playbook for this year. Cal's is from last year. I wanted to make sure we had the same set of plays."

Will glared at Cal. "Sheesh, man, the guy was trying to help! Why'd you jump all over him?"

"But he—I didn't—oh, never mind!" Cal gave up. To his relief, his mother drove up just then. Cal jumped into the car quickly and pretended to fiddle with his seat belt so he wouldn't have to see the disgusted looks on his teammates' faces.

7

Cal did his best to forget the whole play-book incident. Luckily, by the next day none of the players who had witnessed it seemed to think it was worth worrying about. Will Bishop greeted Cal as usual before practice, setting his gear bag down and chatting as if nothing strange had happened.

Cal looked around to see where Jordan was. He spotted him walking toward Mr. Jennings's office. Something about the way he was moving—hesitantly, as if he was afraid to face the coach—made Cal pause and listen.

"Coach, I—I have some bad news," he

overheard Jordan say haltingly. "I lost my binder."

Cal sat on the bench and began to tie his laces. But his attention was fully on the scene unfolding in the office.

"My folks took me out to dinner last night," Jordan explained. "I was studying the plays while waiting for my meal. When my food came, I put the playbook under my chair and"—Jordan's voice dropped so low that Cal had to strain to hear what he said next—"I forgot to grab it when we left. I made my parents take me back to find it, but it was gone."

"I see," the coach said.

"I wanted to check the Dumpsters, but my mother wouldn't let me!" Jordan said. "It kills me, thinking of it buried under old salad and hamburger buns!"

Mr. Jennings was silent for a long moment. Then Cal heard the squeak of a chair as the coach rose to his feet. "Well, I'm disappointed, to say the least. But I appreciate your honesty. And I have to agree with your mother on this one. I wouldn't have wanted you diving into Dumpsters after it, either. I'll make you another copy."

"Oh, no, sir, I can do that! I just wanted to let you know," Jordan said quickly. "Look, there's Will. I'll ask him if I can borrow his tonight."

He stepped out of the office, followed by Mr. Jennings. "Hey, Will, can I take your playbook for a night, so I can make a copy of it?"

Will shook his head. "Sorry, man, I left mine at home today." Then he jerked a thumb at Cal. "Why don't you borrow Cal's instead?"

"Mine?" Cal said, startled. "Why mine?"

Will shrugged. "You said you already know all the plays."

"That's right, you did say that," Jordan agreed. "So you don't need it. Unless... well, unless you don't really know them?"

Cal felt trapped. He certainly didn't want to give Jordan his annotated playbook. Yet refusing the request would make him look as though he'd been lying about his knowledge of the plays. That wouldn't be good with Mr. Jennings standing right there; he had just made it very clear that he valued truthfulness.

So, with great reluctance, Cal pulled the binder from his duffel bag and handed it to Jordan. As he did, he was sure he detected a triumphant gleam in the seventh grader's eye.

"Thanks, man. I'll just give it right to Mr. Jennings when I'm done with it, okay?" Jordan patted the binder's cover. "I'm sure the information in here will come in handy."

Something in the way he said it made Cal turn cold. He suddenly wished he had time to erase all his notes. But instead he watched mutely as Jordan shoved the binder into his locker, slammed the door, and twirled the combination.

Cal didn't have time to worry about the binder anymore then, for practice was about to begin. Before warm-ups, Mr. Jennings made an announcement.

"We'll be holding tryouts for team kicker and punter after practice on Friday. If you're interested in that or in place holding, sign up on the sheet posted outside my office by Thursday afternoon. Thursday afternoon will also be when I announce the starting lineup for our first game, which is against the Leopards on Monday."

He waited for the excited murmurs to die down before continuing. "That match is coming up quickly, so for the rest of the week, we'll be working hard to get our offense running like clockwork and our defense blocking with power and control. I expect to see top effort from all of you, every time you set foot onto this field. Now start with a few laps."

As Cal jogged around the gridiron, he

listened to the chatter about the upcoming game. He was psyched for it, too, as it would most likely be the first real test of his quarterbacking skills.

But as he rounded a corner, he was suddenly struck by a thought so horrible that he nearly tripped.

I might not be the starting quarterback. Mr. Jennings might choose Jordan instead of me!

The very idea made his stomach churn. How would he feel if it actually happened?

Humiliated, that's how!

Then he took a deep breath and replaced the bad thought with one of determination. *I'll just have to make sure that I perform better than Jordan this week. Starting now!*

And with that, he picked up his pace.

8

True to his word, Mr. Jennings worked the team hard that day. He took the defense to one end of the field, while Coach Owen and Coach Lukas took Cal, Jordan, and the rest of the offense to the other.

Coach Lukas took charge of the drill. "We'll be working on a few running plays today," he said. "Those of you returning from last year should remember the first one, the trap play. Who knows it?"

Cal's hand shot into the air. "It's a basic run up the middle," he said when Coach Lukas nodded at him to answer. "We set up in the I formation: seven offensive linemen with a wide receiver on the right a few yards back from the line. I stand right behind the center, with the fullback and tailback stacked behind me."

Coach Lukas looked satisfied, but Coach Owen raised an eyebrow. "*You* stand right behind the center?" he said in a mocking tone. "Don't you mean the *quarterback?* Or have you forgotten there's another quarterback contender on the Hurricanes?"

Cal shot a look at Jordan, whose hand seemed to be covering a smirk. "N-no," he stammered. "I mean, yes, I meant *quarterback,* and no, I haven't forgotten about Jordan." *How could I?* he added silently.

"And how does the play unfold?"

Coach Lukas's question was directed at Cal. Cal thought for a moment, picturing the page from the playbook. "After the snap, the linemen open a gap to the center's immediate right. The fullback blocks, too, hitting the defender to the center's left. His movement is designed to fool the defense into thinking the play is to the left. But it's really to the right, which is where the tailback carries the ball after I—that is, after the *quarterback*," he corrected with a quick glance at Coach Owen, "hands off to him."

"Very good," Coach Lukas said. "Since you know the play, you'll QB to start. Head to the 20-yard line. Now let's see how many of you were paying attention to Cal's description of the play. Coach Owen?"

As Cal hustled to the line, Coach Owen rattled off several names and positions, instructing those players to hit the field, too. Soon the lineup was set. Center Will Bishop was flanked by guards Ryan Lee and Scott Zito. Outside of them were tackles Kevin Flanders and Troy Tetrault, with Ian Bailey at tight end on the right and a burly seventh grader named David Barr in the same position on the left. Fred Hawkins was at wide receiver. Running backs Mario and Raul Torrez completed the lineup.

As the twins jogged toward him, helmets under their arms, Cal tried not to stare. It wasn't easy. He was fascinated by how exactly alike they looked, both dark-haired with piercing black eyes, thick eyebrows, snub noses, and olive-toned skin. In fact, the only obvious difference in their appearance was their jersey numbers.

However, while they were identical in looks, Cal knew from experience that there were differences in how they moved. Raul was faster off the mark than Mario. His speed often gave him a one-step advantage over the defense, which led to crucial gains. Mario, on the other hand, was much more agile than Raul, able to pick up yardage by quickly changing direction and evading tackles. Cal had noted these differences in his playbook as *Raul = faster* and *Mario = maneuvers better*.

Before the play began, the coaches set up orange cones to indicate the positions of the defense. Five cones formed a tight front line, with five others, more widely spaced and behind the first row, standing in for three linebackers and two cornerbacks. The eleventh cone, representing the free safety, was set far back and in the middle of the field.

"All right, people, listen up," Coach Owen barked. The players quieted immediately. "Here's what we want to happen."

He began pantomiming the play. "The center snaps to the QB. Immediately after the snap—and I mean *immediately*—you blockers *move.*"

He then pointed to everyone in turn except Cal and Raul and indicated which defender each player should block. Except for Ryan Lee, who had to cut sharply from Will's left to hit the tackle to Will's right, most of the blocks were directed at the defenders in front of them.

Coach Owen turned to Raul. "If those guys do their jobs, there will be a hole a mile wide just to Will's right. You get that hand-off and punch right through that hole."

Raul nodded.

"Then let's make it happen." He clapped loudly and ordered the players to their positions.

The linemen got into their three-point stances, feet shoulder-width apart and fingertips of one hand braced on the turf in front of them. Cal stood behind Will, his knees bent and his hands splayed open with his thumbs together. When he was ready for the snap, he called out the play.

Will thrust the ball into his hands. The linemen exploded into action, each one making for his cone defender. Cal stepped back and pivoted. At the same time, Raul surged forward, holding his arms and hands parallel to the ground and separated just inches apart to create a pocket at his midsection.

When Raul reached him, Cal shoved the ball right into that pocket, releasing it when he felt Raul's hands close around it. Then he danced away and watched as Raul charged through the hole next to Will.

Coach Lukas blew his whistle and waved them back into position. "Again!" he called.

The Hurricanes offense repeated the trap play several more times. The coaches tinkered a little with the lineup, switching Mario and Raul and subbing Juan for Fred. Although his own role in the play was very straightforward, Cal didn't get bored doing it over and over. The repetition was helping him build muscle memory; when the time came to do the play in a game, he'd be more likely to perform his part automatically.

After a while, Coach Owen sent Cal to the sidelines so Jordan could take a turn. Cal hoped that Jordan would muff the play, but the seventh grader did just what he was supposed to do.

"Looks like you've got yourself some real competition for the starting QB slot," Fred said from his spot next to Cal on the bench.

"It's just one play," Cal muttered. "It's not like Jordan's done anything spectacular out there."

"True," Fred agreed, and took a long drink from his water bottle. "Of course," he added, "you haven't, either. Well, looks like I'm going back in. See you out there." He tossed his bottle aside and hurried onto the field.

Cal stared after him, digesting what he had just said. Fred was right; except for remembering what the trap play was, he hadn't done anything to set him above Jordan.

But what more can I do?

The answer to that question didn't come to him until Thursday afternoon. The team had continued working on the trap play during the practices, adding the defense to make it more like a real game situation. They'd also worked on two other running plays. The first was a sweep from a wing T formation that saw a running back moving laterally from left to right for the handoff and then racing through a gap on the far right. The other was a blast from a wishbone setup that could be run either to the right or to the left of the center. The offense had little trouble when the blast was to the right but faltered when they tried it to the left.

"We'll go over that more tomorrow," Mr. Jennings said when practice ended for the day. Then he reminded them about tryouts for kicker. "We'll need a place holder, too, don't forget."

Cal had shared place-holding duties with Charlie Nielsen last year. It was an easy-enough job—so long as the kicker didn't connect with the holder's hand instead of the ball—and he had already put his name on the list for the job again this year.

But until that moment he hadn't considered testing his skill at kicking.

Why shouldn't I, though? he mused. *Mr. Jennings said that effort counts for a lot in his book. So even if I'm terrible, I'll have shown him and the other coaches that I'm willing to go the extra mile. And if I do succeed, then I'm that much more valuable to the team.*

Any way he looked at it, it was a win-win situation. So, after he showered, Cal added his name to the list of players on the kicker sign-up sheet.

9

Cal slept like a log Thursday night. He woke up refreshed and raring to go. He didn't even mind that he had to get through a day of school before hitting the gridiron.

"Hey, Raul! How's it going, man?" he called out when he spotted the Torrez twin in the hallway the next morning. "Ready for another intense workout this afternoon?"

"You know it!" Raul answered with a grin. "And I know something else, too. If we keep playing like we've been playing, those Leopards better watch their spots on Monday!"

"You got that right!" The two bumped fists and then hurried off to their classes.

Cal was still feeling charged up when he entered the locker room later that afternoon. He wasn't even bothered when he saw Jordan poring over his playbook.

That changed a moment later, however. Cal was on his way to the bathroom when he noticed Jordan heading to Mr. Jennings's office with the binder. A few seconds later, he came out empty-handed, shutting the door behind him so that it locked with a click.

Guess he's finally done with it, Cal thought. He figured Jordan would go to his locker to get ready for practice then. But instead, Jordan looked around as if searching for someone. Then he made a beeline toward the Torrez twins.

Curious, Cal ducked out of sight into the bathroom to listen to their conversation.

"Hey, guys, you sure looked strong out there this week," Jordan said. Then he chuckled. "You know, it's a good thing you two wear different numbers, or I'd be getting you confused all the time!"

Raul laughed. "Trust me, you wouldn't be the only one. Even people we've known all our lives sometimes mix us up."

Jordan laughed, too. "Yeah, I bet that's why Cal had to make so many notes about you in his playbook. You know, so he could keep you guys straight in his mind."

Dead silence followed that statement.

"He wrote about us?" one of the twins said at last, his tone incredulous.

"What did he say?" the other one demanded to know.

Cal knew he hadn't written anything nasty about the twins—but something told him Jordan would find a way to make it seem like he had.

He was right.

"Oh, boy, I probably shouldn't tell you," Jordan said hesitantly, "but, um, he said that Mario was slow and…"

"And?"

"And that Raul couldn't maneuver very well," Jordan finished, his voice laced with misery.

Cal wanted to charge out of the bathroom to explain that he had written no such thing, that his exact words were that Raul was faster and Mario maneuvered better. But how could he? He'd first have to admit he'd just been eavesdropping. Then he'd have to confess that he had, in fact, written about their skills. Based on their reactions, they weren't likely to appreciate that confession. And finally, he had no proof of what he'd actually written, for the book was locked away in Mr. Jennings's office.

"What else did he write?" Mario asked angrily.

"Nothing! At least, not about you," Jordan amended.

"Meaning he wrote stuff about other Hurricanes, too? Let me see that book!"

71

"I can't!" Jordan said. "I just turned it in to the coach." He let out a moan. "Oh, man, Cal is going to kill me when you confront him about this."

Raul snorted. "Don't worry, we won't say a word."

"And if anyone is going to be killed," Mario added, smacking a fist into his palm, "it's going to be *him*, not you. Where is he, anyway?"

Cal backed into one of the bathroom stalls and quietly closed the door. He sat on the toilet seat, pulling his feet up so no one would know he was there.

What am I going to do? he thought frantically. *And what are* they *going to do?*

He waited in the bathroom until he heard the locker room go quiet. Then he hurried out to the field.

"About time," Coach Owen said with an exaggerated look at his watch.

"Sorry! I—I couldn't find my mouth

guard. I knew I wouldn't be allowed to play without it. But see? I found it!" Cal knew he was babbling. To stop himself, he held up the plastic mold of his upper teeth.

Coach Owen eyed the mouth guard with distaste. "Charming. Now put it in and join the others for laps."

Cal was a quarter of a lap behind the rest of the team. Feeling conspicuous, he picked up his pace, only to slow down again when he realized Jordan and the twins were in front of him. Jogging with them was Will Bishop. That they were at the back of the pack was strange because they were among the fastest kids on the team. Then he had a sudden suspicion as to why they were hanging back together.

They're talking about me.

His suspicion was confirmed when Will glanced over his shoulder and growled, "Pipe down, he's sneaking up behind us."

Cal suddenly flashed on another page in

the playbook. He wasn't remembering the play outlined there, however. Rather, it was something he'd noted about Will— something about how Will occasionally rushed the snap in his eagerness to make his block. He suspected Jordan had told Will about that note and that Will, like the twins, hadn't taken kindly to Cal's observation.

After the warm-ups, Mr. Jennings put the players right to work running through the trap play. He named Cal as the quarterback, something that would have delighted Cal just the day before. But today, he hurried to his position with a feeling of dread, recalling what the twins had said about "killing" him. He didn't think they'd actually harm him in any way, but he couldn't help wondering how they'd exact their revenge.

He found out during the first runthrough of the trap play. After the snap, Cal pivoted and stuck the ball in Raul's waiting hands. To his surprise, Raul bobbled the handoff.

"Come on, Cal," Raul complained loudly. "That handoff was way up here!" He pointed to a spot high on his chest. "How am I supposed to get a good grip on the ball if you jam it in my throat?"

Cal knew for a fact that he had stuck the ball in Raul's midsection, not his upper chest. He didn't correct Raul, however. Instead, he swallowed his retort, returned to his position behind Will, and called out the play again.

That's when Will made his move. Instead of shoving the ball neatly into Cal's waiting hands, he gave it a sharp twist just as it hit Cal's palms. As a result, Cal dropped the ball.

Fweet!

Coach Owen's whistle shrilled. "What'd you do, grease your hands before practice?"

"Sorry," Cal muttered over his teammates' titters.

He set up again. This time, the snap was sound. He rose quickly and pivoted to make the handoff. Suddenly, he felt a stabbing pain in his right calf. A second later, Raul sprawled on the ground next to him.

"Dude, what is your problem? You totally tripped me!" Raul cried.

Cal couldn't take it anymore. "I did not!" he protested. "You ran into me!"

Raul got to his feet, his eyes narrowing dangerously. "Are you suggesting that I'm not capable of maneuvering around you?" He took a step toward Cal. "Is that what you're suggesting?"

Before Cal could say another word, someone tapped him on the shoulder. He whirled around to find Jordan standing behind him. "What?" he snapped.

Jordan jerked a thumb toward the sidelines. "Coach says I'm in. And you"—he gave a slow smile—"are out."

10

Cal stormed to the sidelines and threw himself onto the bench. Any guilt he had felt at the beginning of practice had been replaced by fury. That fury grew as he watched Jordan successfully execute the play he himself had failed to complete.

"Having an off day?" someone said.

Cal looked up to see Coach Lukas studying him. "You could say that," he muttered.

"Well, let's see if we can change that. Come on. Mr. Jennings told me to work with you on your handoff so you're ready when you go back in."

Cal huffed out a breath. "Don't you mean *if* I go back in?"

"No," the coach replied simply. "I mean when. Come on."

Cal followed him to an open section of the field. Coach Lukas tossed him a ball. "On my mark, pretend you've taken the snap. I'll run toward you, and you make the handoff. Ready? Go!"

Feeling a little foolish, Cal crouched low and mimed getting the snap. When he heard footfalls coming from behind him, he pivoted, sighted the coach's open arms, and thrust the ball between them. The coach grasped the ball, shifted it under one arm, and danced a few steps forward before stopping.

"Nothing wrong with that handoff," he said. "Again."

Coach Lukas worked with Cal for several minutes, coming at him from different angles and at different speeds. A few times, he held his arms up higher to mimic a tall player and at other times down low as if he were short. Cal easily adjusted to each change.

Finally, the coach called a halt. "As far as I can tell, there's nothing wrong with your technique. So I wonder why you were having such troubles before."

He seemed to expect an answer, but Cal wasn't about to admit that his teammates had purposefully made him look bad; doing so would mean giving a full explanation of why they were mad. Instead, he simply thanked the coach for helping him work out the kinks.

"Not a problem," Coach Lukas replied. "You've got sound fundamentals. Now trade places with Jordan, and put them to use."

As it turned out, Mario, Raul, and Will were replaced by seventh graders at the same time Cal took over for Jordan. The new players wore similar expressions:

determined yet a bit apprehensive. Cal remembered feeling the same way last year, wanting to perform well yet fearing that he'd make a mistake.

He also remembered something Charlie Nielsen had once told him: "When you're the quarterback, you're the leader on the field. You have to be confident, but more important, you have to show confidence in your teammates. If you do, they'll trust themselves to make the play."

Cal acted on that advice now, shouting encouragement to the younger players between plays, applauding when they performed well, and assuring them that they'd get it right next time when they messed up. His chatter boosted the energy on the field, and after several run-throughs, they were working together like a well-oiled machine.

"I like what I see out there!" Mr. Jennings shouted after their fifth successful execution of the sweep play. "Let's see if the boys on the sidelines can do as well."

He waved the first line back onto the field. Jordan started to join them but stopped when the coach told Cal to keep playing.

Cal felt a moment of intense satisfaction at the look of frustration he saw cross Jordan's face then. But as Mario, Raul, and Will returned to the lineup, he wondered if he'd soon be the one wearing that expression. The threesome seemed to have decided that they'd proved their point, however—or else they feared their little tricks might be detected, for they didn't pull any more fast ones on him for the rest of the afternoon.

When practice ended, Mr. Jennings called the team together to announce the starting roster for the game against the Leopards. Cal waited anxiously as the coach went through his list.

"And finally, quarterback," Mr. Jennings said at last. "This was a tough call because both Jordan and Cal have performed well. But for Monday's game, we're going to start Cal."

Cal let out a long breath of relief. No doubt Jordan would see plenty of playing time against the Leopards, but at least he wouldn't be on the field first!

With the roster set, Mr. Jennings told the players it was time for kicking tryouts. "We'll take it in three rounds. The first kick is off the tee. The second is a punt. The third will be with a place holder." He beckoned to Cal. "Since you have experience place holding, would you mind doing it for the others after you kick?"

"No problem," Cal said. Then he hurried to join the line forming behind the tee. To his dismay, Jordan was already in that line. He tried to ignore him, but the seventh grader immediately turned around.

"Congratulations on making starting QB. You deserve it," he said. He nudged the player in front of him. "Don't you think so, Scott?"

The guard nodded. "Absolutely. I mean, you did well, Jordan, but Cal, you've got more experience. Plus, you put in your time last year, learning the ropes. If Coach Fredericks were still here, you'd start every game, no question."

A fleeting look of sourness crossed Jordan's face. But then he grinned and said, "Well, I guess I'm lucky that Coach Fredericks isn't here, because maybe I've still got a shot!"

Scott shrugged. "Yeah, maybe. But don't be surprised if you start most of the games on the bench." With that, he stepped forward to take his turn.

Jordan didn't say anything more to Cal before taking his kick. The ball flew high, but not far. Cal didn't do much better with the tee, the punt, or the placekick, either, but he didn't care. He was still glowing with happiness at what Scott had said.

Maybe I've been worrying over nothing, he thought as he held the ball in place for the next kicker, Zack Tarnell. Zack played soccer in the spring and had a cannon for a leg, which he used now to send the ball soaring through the uprights. His other two kicks had been just as powerful and true.

Ian Bailey, who was next in line, just shook his head. "Gentlemen, I think we have a winner!" he said, stepping aside without even bothering to take his kick. Scott and two other players did the same.

Jordan did not. He fixed a steely gaze on Cal, a humorless smile on his lips. Then he took a step, planted his left foot, and drew back his right.

In that instant, Cal had a premonition.

He's going to kick my hand!

11

The second the thought hit his brain, Cal's body reacted; he jerked the football away.

Swish! Thud!

Jordan's foot struck nothing but air. His leg flew up. Off balance, he fell to the turf, landing hard on his back. He lay there, groaning.

Mr. Jennings and the assistant coaches rushed up. "What happened?" Coach Lukas asked.

"He—he yanked the ball," Jordan said weakly.

Coach Owen rounded on Cal. "Why on earth did you do that?" he demanded.

"I thought he was going to kick my hand," Cal mumbled.

"He could have been seriously hurt, you know!" the assistant coach snapped.

Jordan struggled to a sitting position, his eyes wide and teary. "My foot never even got close to the ball!" he protested. "You pulled it away too soon for that!"

"All right, all right," Mr. Jennings said. He gave Jordan the once-over. "You just got the wind knocked out of you. So up you go." He helped Jordan to his feet.

Cal got up, too, hoping to explain that he'd never pulled the ball from a kicker before this moment. But the coach didn't seem to be interested. "Just be sure it doesn't happen in a game" was all he said.

Tryouts ended with Zack being named the team's kicker. Cal followed his teammates into the locker room, feeling the eyes of several on him as he walked to his locker to collect his belongings.

I didn't do it on purpose! he wanted to scream. But he didn't think anyone would believe him, not when Jordan was the one who'd gotten hurt.

After his strenuous week at school and at football practice, Cal was looking forward to a weekend of relaxation and video games. But his parents had other ideas.

"Time to spread the mulch in the flower beds!" his mother announced brightly first thing Saturday morning.

A truck delivered a huge pile of richly scented shredded wood a little while later. For the next several hours, Cal and his sisters manned the shovels, his father hefted the wheelbarrow loads, and his mother raked the mulch into smooth layers.

"Why do we have so much landscaping?" Tracy groaned during a snack break. "This is taking forever!"

"We should just pave the whole yard," Cal grumbled.

"No way!" his younger sister, Monica, disagreed. "Then we'd spend our whole winter shoveling snow!"

Finally, the enormous pile had dwindled to just a small mound. When the last shovelful had been spread, Mrs. Kelliher declared it a job well done. "Pizza for dinner," she added, "although my arms are so tired one of you might have to feed me!"

After their hard day's work on Saturday, the Kellihers all took it easy Sunday morning. Cal's mother and father sat at the dining room table, sipping coffee and reading the newspaper, while Cal played a video game and his sisters squared off for several rounds of their favorite board game.

Later, they all got into the car to visit Cal's grandparents, who lived in the next town over. Cal loved talking to Grandpa Matt, who, like Cal and his father, had played football as a teenager. They wound up staying for a supper of spaghetti and meatballs, returning home well after dark.

Cal was sleepy from the good food and long weekend, but before he went to bed, he checked to make sure his uniform was in his duffel bag. He found his mouth guard, too, and gave it a quick cleaning with his toothbrush and toothpaste. Then he snapped it back inside its case, zipped it into a small outside pocket of the duffel, and went to bed.

He awoke before his alarm the next morning. The day was bright and clear, the air crisp and scented like a fresh fall apple. It was an easy Monday for Cal, no tests or quizzes or major assignments, which was lucky because his mind was on the upcoming game and not his schoolwork. When the final bell rang, he hurried to the locker room to suit up and go through his pregame ritual.

Like many athletes, Cal was superstitious.

Some players made sure to eat the same meal before every game or to wear a particular pair of underwear or socks, believing it gave them good luck.

Cal's ritual didn't involve food or clothing but a special question he'd learned from his father, who had learned it from Grandpa Matt. Before every game, he splashed his face with cold water from the third sink in the boys' locker room. Then he stared at his reflection for three seconds while asking himself, *Who do you want to see staring back at you after the game, a winner or a loser?*

The answer to the rhetorical question was obvious, of course. Yet, somehow, asking it always made Cal more determined to help the Hurricanes win. Last year he mainly helped by cheering them on from the bench. But this year, it was different. He was the starting quarterback. Instead of following the action from the sidelines or coming in so Charlie could rest, he would be right in the thick of things from the very beginning. Just as he had once looked to Charlie to lead the team to victory, now his teammates would be looking to him.

He was one of the first players to arrive in the locker room that afternoon. He changed quickly, stuffing his clothes into his empty duffel and putting his mouth guard on the bench next to his water bottle. Then he went to the bathroom, where he dawdled until Troy, who was taking his time in a stall, left. Only when he was alone did he go through his ritual.

Who do you want to see staring back at you after the game, a winner or a loser?

He hadn't been out of the locker area for more than a few minutes, but in his absence most of the other Hurricanes had arrived. The atmosphere was charged with excited energy as the boys joked, whooped, and jabbed one another playfully.

Juan Morales had taken the locker next to his. "What'd you do, take a shower *before* the game?" he asked with a glance at Cal's damp face.

"Nah, I jumped through a sprinkler on the way in," Cal replied with a smile. He moved his water bottle so he could sit down.

That was when he noticed his mouth guard was missing.

12

Cal frowned. He bent forward and looked under and around the bench. The mouth guard wasn't on the floor.

Okay, don't panic, he told himself. *Maybe you only thought you took it out of your duffel.*

He unzipped the pocket where he'd stowed the case the night before. It was empty. With mounting dread, he turned his duffel inside out, searching in every pouch, pocket, and fold.

"What's the matter?" Juan asked, eyeing him curiously.

"I—I can't find my mouth guard," Cal said.

"Well, you better find it," Juan said, "or else you won't be able to play!"

"I know, I know!" Cal said, his voice rising. "I put it right here before I went to the bathroom. I know I did! You didn't see it? It's a blue case with *Cal* written on it!"

He looked all through his locker, his pants pockets, and his school backpack. Nothing!

Juan shoved a cell phone at him. "Maybe you left it at home. Call your mom and have her bring it!"

But Cal waved the phone away. "It's no use. It's gone." He sank down onto the bench, head in hands.

"Tough break, Cal," Juan said sympathetically. "I guess that means Jordan will be quarterbacking today. I hope he's up for it."

"Why wouldn't he be?" Cal wanted to know.

"He just told me he's really nervous about coming off the bench. So now that he'll be starting—"

"What do you mean, he just told you?" Cal interrupted sharply. "He was here? Where is he now?"

Juan shrugged. "I don't know. He was here when I went to fill my water bottle. When I got back, he was gone."

Cal's mind whirled. He could see the scene in his mind clear as day: Jordan coming to talk to Juan, spotting the blue case with Cal's name on it, Juan leaving—and Jordan pocketing the mouth guard, knowing that Cal wouldn't be allowed to play without it.

It was just a gut feeling. Cal had no way of proving his suspicions about Jordan. Juan hadn't seen anything, not even the case itself. Without a witness, what was Cal to do, go to Mr. Jennings and demand a search of Jordan's belongings?

Mr. Jennings. Cal groaned. *What's he going to say when I tell him I don't have my mouth guard?*

The coach didn't say anything, not at first, but his expression made it very clear that he was displeased. "I don't have time to babysit you players," he finally said. "I expect you to be responsible for your equipment."

Cal was about to apologize when Jordan suddenly appeared in the office doorway.

"Hey, Mr. Jennings, I have a quick question about jazz band—oh, sorry, I didn't see you there, Cal. I'll talk to you after the game, sir." He started to leave, but the coach stopped him.

"Jordan, come in and sit down."

Looking mystified, Jordan did as he was told.

"What's up, sir?"

"Seems you'll be starting at quarterback today instead of Cal," Mr. Jennings replied wearily.

"What? Why?"

Mr. Jennings rubbed his eyes. "Cal doesn't have his mouth guard."

Jordan's eyes widened. "You mean he won't be able to play today? Not at all? What if I lend him one of my mouth guards? My mom gets me two every season, just in case I lose one," he added, addressing Cal. "Guess it makes sense. Maybe you should think about doing the same thing."

Mr. Jennings shook his head. "A generous gesture, Jordan, but too unsanitary, I'm afraid. No, you're our starter—and our finisher for today."

Word of the quarterback switch spread like wildfire through the locker room. Cal felt his teammates' sidelong glances as they gathered for the pregame pep talk.

"The Hurricanes beat the Leopards twice last year," Mr. Jennings said. "If you play with the energy and determination you demonstrated all last week, I'm confident that you can beat them again. Remember, it will be a total team effort. Everyone will have a chance to play.

"Everyone who is eligible to play, that is," he added with a sharp glance at Cal.

The team took to the field with a loud, enthusiastic roar. The game began immediately after warm-ups. The Hurricanes won the toss and elected to receive. Cal watched the kickoff, but he stared at his feet when the offense took to the field because he couldn't bear to watch Jordan play. Only when he heard a shout did he look up at the action.

From what he could tell, the Hurricanes had moved only a few yards in their first two plays. Now Jordan was fading back for a long pass to try to make up the distance needed for first down. Juan was the intended receiver. He darted straight down the sidelines and then cut sharply to the center, a defender right on his heels. Jordan threw. The ball spiraled high in the air—and landed in Juan's outstretched hands!

Juan spun away from his defender and began running. He chewed up twelve yards before he was tackled. Those yards were just enough for first down. Three plays later, the Hurricanes were on the board with seven points.

To the team's delight and Cal's dismay, Jordan continued to play well. But the Leopards were no pushovers. Whenever the Hurricanes scored, the Leopards answered with a touchdown of their own—until the fourth quarter, when the Hurricanes added seven more points to their side in the final minutes. The Leopards simply ran out of time. Final score: Hurricanes 35, Leopards 28.

The mood in the locker room was jubilant after the win. Jordan was roundly praised by all, including the assistant coaches, for his performance.

"Aw, come on, I didn't win the game single-handedly," the seventh grader said modestly from his spot near the office. "To me, this team is like an orchestra, you know? I may be the conductor"—he pointed around at the boys listening—"but you all make the music!"

"Well put," said Mr. Jennings.

Cal had seen the coach standing in the office doorway, listening to Jordan's speech with a bemused expression. He was positively certain Jordan knew he was there, too.

Jordan, however, whirled around as if startled. Then he pointed at Mr. Jennings but addressed the players. "Did I say I was the conductor? Not true! He's the one who leads us! Am I right?"

Whoops and applause greeted this statement.

"And speaking of music," Jordan added, turning back to Mr. Jennings, "I still have a question to ask you about the jazz band. I'm having trouble with one part of the audition piece. I wondered if I could meet with you before school tomorrow to go over it."

Mr. Jennings nodded. "Certainly. I'll see you in the music room at seven. Good game today, by the way."

"Well, sir, as I've said before, I have you to thank for my improvement!"

Cal listened with disgust. How could Mr. Jennings not see through Jordan? But he didn't; that was clear. It was also clear that from now on, Jordan would most likely be his starting quarterback. If the game today hadn't sealed the spot for him, his fawning and flattery undoubtedly would!

13

Convinced that Jordan would be Mr. Jennings's first choice for starting quarterback from now on, Cal gave less than one hundred percent in the practices that followed Monday's game.

Why bother? he thought whenever Coach Lukas or one of his teammates looked at him in disappointment. *It won't make a difference.*

He was surprised, therefore, to discover how upset he was when, after Friday's practice, Jordan was named the starter for their game against the Chargers. He couldn't figure out why it bothered him so much.

Then, that night, it came to him. He was brushing his teeth before going to bed. After he spit and rinsed, he stared at his reflection for a long time. Staring back at him was a loser.

Cal lay awake for a long time that night, thinking about the tricks Jordan had pulled on him to get what he wanted. *It's like he's blitzed me. He's gone on the offensive, so I'm on the defensive. But what can I do about it?*

Finally he gave up trying to sleep, tossed the covers off, and crossed the room to his desk. He clicked on his laptop, making sure his door was shut tight so the glow wouldn't alert his parents that he was awake. Once the computer booted up, he went to his Internet home page and typed in an address he knew by heart. Moments later, a video-sharing website popped open with his chosen video queued up to play. He muted the volume and then clicked the play button and sat back to watch.

The clip was of his trick play from the last game of the previous season. It was almost comical viewing it with the sound off. Without hearing the coach hiss "go," it looked as if Cal had been stung by a bee when he first took off running for the end zone. He watched it again, pausing the clip to study the face of the shocked Charger, who he now knew was Coach Owen's little brother.

It sure caught him off guard, he thought, staring at the wide O of the boy's mouth. He moved the cursor back and forth so that his image ran in reverse and then sped up in fast-forward. While he felt bad about the effect the play had had on the guy, he still couldn't help marveling that the maneuver had actually worked.

The element of surprise, he thought. *It worked because no one expected me to do what I did.*

Suddenly, he sat up straighter. "No one

expected me to do what I did," he repeated in an excited whisper. He turned off the computer and got back into bed, his mind racing.

So far, Jordan's been the one doing the unexpected. At least, I haven't anticipated any of his moves. He flipped over onto his stomach and put his head on his hands. *But what if I turn the tables? What if I do the unexpected and take him by surprise?*

He went over every trick Jordan had played on him, from the jersey to the likely theft of the mouth guard. He wondered if he could try the same sort of maneuver on Jordan, but he shook the thought away as soon as it entered.

Don't sink to his level, he told himself. *Not if you want to see a winner in the mirror ever again.*

An image of Charlie Nielsen popped into his head then. Charlie was a winner, on and off the football field. He was an all-around decent guy who had gone out of his way to help Cal improve his game last year so that Cal would be ready to step into Charlie's cleats.

I wonder what Jordan would do if I started treating him the way Charlie treated me? He grinned in the darkness as he imagined how bewildered Jordan would be by his sudden overture of friendship. He wasn't sure if doing so would make one bit of difference—*but one thing's for sure: It would take him by surprise!*

Cal decided to test out his new approach that Monday. Ever since that first day in the cafeteria, when he'd spotted Jordan making fun of him, Cal had avoided the eighth-grade football table. Now he made a beeline for it, plunking himself down between the Torrez twins and across from Jordan.

"Hey, guys," he said jovially. "How's it going?"

All conversation stopped. Mario and Raul stared at him from either side, reminding Cal of matching bookends. "Uh, we're fine, thanks," Mario finally answered. "How are you, Cal?"

"I'm getting psyched for the game today, that's how I am," Cal replied with a wide smile. He turned his attention to Jordan. "By the way, I never congratulated you for keeping the Hurricanes' undefeated streak alive. Guess I was too busy acting like a sore loser. But hey, well done, bro!"

He held out a fist. After a moment's hesitation, Jordan bumped it with his own, murmuring "thanks" in a puzzled voice.

Cal dug his sandwich out of his lunch bag and began eating. "So, Jordan, how's your piece for the jazz band audition coming along? I remember you telling Mr. Jennings you needed help with it."

"Um, it's okay," Jordan said.

"Awesome. I wish I knew how to play an

instrument. But I don't have a musical bone in my body." Cal jabbed Raul in the ribs. "Remember that awful piece I made up in sixth grade?"

Raul broke into a grin. "I don't remember it being awful. I remember it being hilarious! What did you get for a grade for that, anyway?"

"You know, it's funny," Cal answered as he finished his sandwich and moved on to his cookie. "I was sure Mr. Jennings would fail me. But I got an A. I guess he appreciated my effort, if not my musical ability."

"*What* musical ability?" Raul joked, earning him another poke in the ribs from Cal.

The lunch bell sounded then, and the boys quickly shoved the last bites of food into their mouths.

"Anyway, good luck with the audition, Jordan, whenever it is," Cal said as he stood up to go. "See you later in the locker room!"

"Hey, Cal, wait for me," Raul said. "I

want to ask you a question about our science lab."

As Cal waited for Raul, he looked back at Jordan. The seventh grader was standing alone at the table. Cal was tempted to turn his back on him. But instead, he waved to him, calling, "Jordan, you coming?"

14

The rest of the school day went by quickly. As usual, Cal was one of the first players to arrive in the locker room. But instead of suiting up right away, he put his gear down and went to find one of the coaches.

"Excuse me, Coach Owen?" he said. "Could I talk to you for a minute?"

The coach nodded. "Yes, Cal, what is it?"

Cal entered the office but didn't sit down. "I was hoping you might do me a favor. Could you—could you tell your brother that I'm sorry for any trouble he had because of that trick play last season? I mean, I'm not sad we won, but until you told me about him, I guess I never really thought about how awful it must have been to be a Charger that day."

Coach Owen was silent for a long moment. "Thank you, Cal," he finally said. "But I'll let you tell him yourself today."

"Huh? But I thought you said—"

The coach smiled. "It took a little, er, *convincing* on my part, but he ended up going out for the team after all."

Cal grinned back. "That's great!"

Now Coach Owen laughed. "I'm glad you think so, although you may change your mind when you meet him on the field. He's grown a lot bigger—and don't forget, I taught him everything he knows!"

"Yikes," Cal said, pretending to shudder. "Thanks for the warning!"

He left then to go suit up. Juan was at his usual locker, and the two chatted about the upcoming game as they dressed. Cal had just tugged his jersey on when he spotted Jordan.

"Hey, Jordan, look!" Cal rummaged in his duffel bag, pulling out not one but two mouth guards. "I decided to take your advice and get a spare. No way both of these can walk away on their own, right?"

"Right," Jordan replied.

"Good luck out there, man," Cal added.

"Yeah, you, too." Jordan gave him a last look and then disappeared into his own row.

Cal turned back to see Juan staring at him.

"You know, I just realized something," Juan said in a low voice. "Remember how you said you left your mouth guard here on the bench before the last game? Well, if you did, then Jordan must have sat down next to it when he came to talk with me. You don't think he...?" He raised his eyebrows questioningly.

"Took it?" Cal said. "Nah! That would be a pretty rotten thing to do!"

"Yeah, it would be," Juan agreed. But he continued to look troubled.

The Hurricanes headed out to the field to begin warming up. The Chargers were there, too. Cal saw Coach Owen talking with one of their players and guessed it was his brother. Cal made a mental note of the boy's uniform number so he could find him after the game.

During the laps, Cal made a point to jog along with Will. Jordan was there, too, and clearly not pleased to see Cal. The younger quarterback opened his mouth to say something, but before any words came out, Cal spoke.

"Hey, Will? I've been meaning to talk to you about something."

"Yeah? What?" the burly center replied gruffly.

"You know how I wrote stuff about you and some of the other guys in my playbook last year?"

Jordan sputtered.

"I didn't do it to be mean or insulting,"

Cal continued, as if Jordan hadn't made a sound. "I made those notes to help me be a better quarterback, so that the team would be stronger."

Will regarded him with surprise. "You did? I—That's not what I heard." He glanced at Jordan, who, Cal saw, was turning beet red, but not from exertion.

"I was afraid of that," Cal said. "Listen, when I get my playbook back at the end of the season, I'd like to show you what I put down so you can see what I meant to do. Okay?"

"Yeah, that'd be fine with me, Cal. Now come on, let's power through the rest of these laps!"

15

The game started ten minutes later. The Chargers won the toss, so Zack Tarnell hurried onto the field with the defense for the kickoff. One solid kick and fair catch later, the Chargers had the ball on their own 22-yard line.

"Here we go, Hurricanes, hold 'em right there!" Cal yelled from the sidelines as the defense took their positions.

Using a series of run plays, the Chargers managed to march fifteen yards down the gridiron on their first possession. They approached the 50-yard line on their first play of the next set of downs. But on the second play, Scott Zito broke free and hammered the ball carrier to the ground for a loss of yards. The Chargers couldn't make up the difference and prepared to punt.

Mario was the Hurricanes punt returner. He caught the ball and immediately began his run.

"Go! Go! Go!" Cal and Raul cried together. Other Hurricanes joined in, their shouts growing louder and more excited as Mario skipped nimbly away from all his attackers. Finally, one Charger stopped him at the Hurricanes 43-yard line.

"You were right, Cal," Raul said just before he ran onto the field. "I don't maneuver as well as Mario does. No way would I have been able to get as far as he just did!"

"Yeah, but you're faster!" Cal called after him. "Now use that speed to fly into the end zone!"

The Hurricanes started off with their basic run play, the trap. Jordan took the snap, pivoted, and handed off to Raul. Will, Ryan, and Scott threw their blocks and punched a hole in the defense to Will's right. Raul didn't hesitate—he zipped through that hole and just kept on going for first down.

Now the Hurricanes had the ball just over the 50-yard line. They gained two yards when they ran the trap to the left. Second down, eight to go. They chewed up five of those eight on the next play. Now they needed just three more to continue.

They got them thanks to Juan. Jordan had called for the sweep. Mario, running from left to right, collected the handoff without a problem, but then he stumbled as he crossed the line of scrimmage. The ball bobbled out of his hands, but, luckily, Juan was there to catch it before it hit the ground. He then managed to dance the extra steps for first down.

Four plays later, the Hurricanes were at the Chargers 9-yard line for first-and-goal.

Then Jordan made a mistake. He'd called for the blast play to the right but must have thought he'd called it to the left, for that's the direction he turned.

"Oh, no!" several Hurricanes moaned on the sidelines.

Mario, the intended receiver, was already heading to the right, unfortunately. Jordan got him the ball by continuing to spin about, but by then Mario was surrounded by defenders. He was taken down easily, buried beneath a pile of Chargers, for a loss of a yard.

Jordan was tackled, too, seconds after he made the handoff. It hadn't seemed like a hard hit to Cal. But as he watched Jordan get up, he sensed something was wrong.

Jordan had been cupping his right wrist. Now he moved his hand aside and stared at the spot. Cal's eyes widened. "Mr. Jennings!" he cried. "Jordan's bleeding!"

"Timeout!" the coach yelled.

Fweet! The referee's whistle blew. All movement on the field halted. The trainer and Mr. Jennings raced over to Jordan.

Jordan didn't seem to want their help. He turned away from them, insisting that he was fine, that it was just a scratch.

The trainer ignored his protests and, with Mr. Jennings's help, herded Jordan to the sidelines. They were joined by a small blond woman who Cal guessed was Jordan's mother. She stood back, silent and anxious, as the trainer ordered Jordan to sit.

"But I'm fine!" Jordan said for the third time.

"Now you listen to me," the trainer said as he began to unroll a long length of bandage around the injury. "You need to sit still so I can help you. You're very lucky. Half an inch to the left and you'd have hit a major artery."

As he wrapped, the trainer told the coach to find whatever it was that had cut Jordan.

"If it's a nail or some kind of rusty metal, he may need to get a tetanus shot," he added, directing his words to Mrs. Stahl. "Regardless, it should be removed so no one else gets hurt."

Jordan finally seemed to resign himself to the situation, for he didn't say another word while his wrist was being bound.

Meanwhile, the players cleared the field so Coach Lukas and Coach Owen could search the area where Jordan had been hurt. Finally, Coach Lukas gave a cry of discovery, bent down, and dislodged a jagged piece of glass that was embedded in the turf. He carried it to the sidelines and showed it the trainer, who grunted and told him to throw it away. The moment Jordan found out he didn't need a shot he said, "Coach, can I go back in?"

"Absolutely not!" his mother said, horrified. "I'm taking you to the emergency room! Not that it doesn't look like you did a fine job," she said with an apologetic glance at the trainer.

"Don't worry, I'd do the same thing," the man assured her.

"But Mom—"

"No buts! The car is right over there. Now come on. I'm sure your teammates can manage without you."

With that, she hustled him to the parking lot, helped him into the car, and drove off.

The referee jogged up to Mr. Jennings then. "How 'bout it, coach? You ready to resume the game?"

"I'm ready," Mr. Jennings replied. He searched the faces of his team, stopping when he reached Cal. "Are you ready, Cal?"

Cal straightened his shoulders and nodded. "I am, sir."

"Then huddle up, boys, and listen to what I want you to do."

16

The Hurricanes rushed back to the line of scrimmage at the Chargers 10-yard line. The Chargers were already there. When the Hurricanes took their positions, the defense quickly moved to cover them. The whistle blew, and the game picked up where it had left off.

The Hurricanes had worked on the play they were about to run all last week. Yet doubt had clouded Cal's teammates' faces when they heard Mr. Jennings's instructions. Cal knew they were thinking of how little effort he'd given that play—all plays— during those practices.

If it's going to work, I have to give them confidence, Cal thought, remembering the advice Charlie had given him the year before. *Confidence in themselves and, more important, confidence in me!*

It was a running play that called for Fred, the wide receiver, to slant to the left and then cut sharply to the right—the number-seven route on the standard passing tree commonly used to outline football plays. If Fred could fool his defender, he'd be wide open when Cal threw him a pass in the far right corner of the end zone.

But would Fred fall into his old habit of looking back too soon? As they ran onto the field, Cal considered reminding him to be careful. Before he could decide, however, Fred jogged up to him and whispered, "Don't worry. I'll wait until the last second!"

"It'll be easy for me to get you the ball, then," Cal whispered back. They grinned at each other and then got into their positions.

Here goes, Cal thought. He set up behind Will and called the play in a loud, clear voice. He took the snap and danced back several steps, praying that the offensive line would hold.

It did. Meanwhile, Fred zipped to the left and then cut to the right. As his feet entered the end zone, he looked back for the pass.

Fred hadn't advertised himself as the receiver—Cal was sure of it. Yet one Charger must have realized where the pass was going, for he rushed to help out his teammate in covering Fred. That should have left a Hurricane free, but if so, Cal couldn't spot him.

But he did spot something else: a hole. Knowing that the defense would surge toward him if he waited any longer, Cal tucked the ball under his arm and ran toward that hole.

I'm going to make it! he thought gleefully. *I'm going to score a touchd—!*

Wham! A defender hit Cal like a ton of bricks, flattening him. Cal felt the ball loosen in his grasp and scrambled to hold on.

"That's for last year," the defender growled with satisfaction. Then he held out a hand to help Cal up.

Cal accepted with a shaky grin. "You must be Coach Owen's brother," he said.

The Charger nodded and then lumbered away to wait for the Hurricanes to set up their next play. Cal had managed to run far enough to bring the ball back to the 10-yard line, but now it was second down.

"So what do we try now?" Juan asked.

"We fake 'em out," Cal said without hesitation. "Raul, you come up on my left. I'll fake it to you. Mario, you take the handoff on my right. Blockers, open a hole for him on Scott's outside shoulder. Ready? Break!"

This time, the play ran like clockwork. The linemen shoved their defenders apart, creating a gap for Mario. Mario charged through and nearly made it into the end zone. Nearly, but not quite. The ball was now on the 1-yard line.

Amid screams of "Hold 'em! Hold 'em!" from the Chargers faithful and yells of "Push it over! Push it over!" from the Hurricanes fans, Cal gathered with his teammates in the huddle.

"Dive play," Cal said. "Handoff to Raul."

"You'll be buried before I can get the ball," Raul objected. "I think you should take it in."

"A QB sneak?" Cal's heart started racing. "I've never done one before, though."

"No time like the present," Raul said.

"We'll give you the hole," Will said, looking at Ryan, the left guard.

Ryan nodded. "All you'll have to do is fall through it for the touchdown."

"Okay, I'll do it," Cal said. "Break!"

They clapped once and separated to their positions.

Here goes nothing! Cal thought. He called the play. The ball hit his hands. He pulled it up and glanced to his left. Like curtains separating to let in a ray of sun, Ryan and Will parted the defense to reveal a patch of open turf. Cal lunged for the gap, thrusting the ball before him as he fell.

Fweet!

"Touchdown!"

Cal was heaved to his feet by his over-joyed teammates and ushered off the field to the sounds of cheers and whoops. Those points weren't game winners—there were still more than three quarters left to play—but Cal knew that no matter what the end result was, when he looked in the mirror after this game, he'd see a winner smiling back at him.

17

Oh, man, that's going to leave one heck of a scar!"

Cal and several other Hurricanes were sitting in the bleachers with Jordan before practice two days later, admiring the stitches Jordan was showing them.

"So how long before you can practice again?" Fred asked.

Jordan shrugged. "The doctor said if everything heals without a problem, then I can come back after the stitches come out." He glanced at Cal. "That means you're starting quarterback for at least the next two games."

A week ago, that statement would have

been delivered with an undercurrent of resentment. But now, Jordan simply said it as the fact that it was. Cal heard it that way, too, instead of as the challenge he might have suspected a week earlier.

The Hurricanes had won the game against the Chargers by a slim margin, just 14 to 7. Their second touchdown had come late in the fourth quarter, on the same pass play to Fred that had failed in the first period. Fred made his catch after completely hoodwinking his defender, which made the touchdown all the sweeter for him.

After the game, Cal heard someone call his name. He turned to find Charlie Nielsen standing by the bleachers. "Hey, Cal, how are you?" his old teammate said. "I caught the last part of the game. You're looking good out there!"

"Thanks, Charlie." They walked together to the locker room, chatting about how their school years had been going so far.

"I've been meaning to get in touch with you since the end of August," Charlie confessed. "But I've been so busy. High school is really different from middle school. The worst part is that I'm one of the little guys again. Some of those juniors and seniors are huge—and that's just the girls!"

He and Cal broke out laughing. Then Charlie said he had to get going. "Listen, though, I still have the gift certificate to the pizza place you gave me. How about we get together this weekend and spend it?"

"That'd be great!"

Charlie promised to call and then left. Cal continued into the locker room, showered, and changed into his regular clothes. He had just passed the office on his way out the door when he paused and turned back.

"Hey, Mr. Jennings, I was wondering if anyone is taking Jordan his stuff. If not, I bet my mom wouldn't mind if we brought it to him now. That way, I could see how he's doing and let him know how we did today."

Mr. Jennings raised an eyebrow. "I have to say I'm a little surprised by the offer. I was under the impression that you and Jordan were, how shall I put this, competitors?"

Cal grinned. "You mean, you thought we didn't like each other. Well, we didn't—and maybe Jordan still doesn't like me. But I decided that if that's ever going to change, one of us is going to have to make the first move." He shrugged. "It might as well be me."

The coach nodded. Then he took out a scrap of paper and jotted down an address. "Here's where he lives. I'll help you get his belongings."

Mr. Jennings located the master locker key and opened Jordan's locker. As Cal pulled out Jordan's duffel, something fell to the floor. He leaned over and picked it up. It was a blue case with a name written on it.

"What's that? Jordan's mouth guard? Better put it in one of his duffel pockets," Mr. Jennings advised. Just then the office phone rang. He went to answer it, leaving Cal staring at the case in his hand.

It was a mouth guard, all right. But the name written on it was *Cal*, not *Jordan*. After a moment, Cal stuck the case in his pocket. He knew he could confront Jordan with it. But what would be the point? Such a confrontation would just cause the rift between them to get bigger, and that would be no good for the team.

Still, he had the satisfaction of knowing his instincts had been right.

Jordan seemed shocked to see Cal at his front door later that afternoon. He shot Cal a sharp look when he saw his duffel— wondering, Cal suspected, about the mouth guard. But Cal kept his expression neutral as he placed the bag in the hallway, giving him a quick recap of the game as he did.

"You know," Cal said, "someone once told me that the Hurricanes would be a better team with two strong quarterbacks. I think he was right. What do you think?"

He hadn't really expected Jordan to eagerly agree, but still, he was disappointed when the only answer he got was a one-shoulder shrug.

"Well, think about it, anyway. See you at school," Cal said. He turned and started down the steps.

"Hey, Cal, before you leave, will you answer one question?"

Cal turned back. "Sure. What is it?"

Jordan gave a lopsided grin. "Do you play basketball? Because I'm going out for the team after football, and I'd like to know who I'm going up against!"

Cal laughed. "One sport at a time, Jordan," he called as he returned to his mother's car. "One sport at a time!"

THE #1 SPORTS SERIES FOR KIDS

MATT CHRISTOPHER®

Read them all!

- Baseball Flyhawk
- Baseball Turnaround
- The Basket Counts
- Body Check
- Catch That Pass!
- Catcher with a Glass Arm
- Center Court Sting
- Centerfield Ballhawk
- Challenge at Second Base
- The Comeback Challenge
- Comeback of the Home Run Kid
- Cool as Ice
- The Diamond Champs
- Dirt Bike Racer
- Dirt Bike Runaway
- Dive Right In

- Double Play at Short
- Face-Off
- Fairway Phenom
- Football Double Threat
- Football Fugitive
- Football Nightmare
- The Fox Steals Home
- Goalkeeper in Charge
- The Great Quarterback Switch
- Halfback Attack*
- The Hockey Machine
- The Home Run Kid Races On
- Hook Shot Hero
- Hot Shot
- Ice Magic
- Johnny Long Legs

*Previously published as *Crackerjack Halfback*

Karate Kick

The Kid Who Only Hit Homers

Lacrosse Face-Off

Lacrosse Firestorm

Long-Arm Quarterback

Long Shot for Paul

Look Who's Playing First Base

Miracle at the Plate

Mountain Bike Mania

Nothin' But Net

Out at Second

Penalty Shot

Power Pitcher**

QB Blitz

Return of the Home Run Kid

Run for It

Shoot for the Hoop

Skateboard Renegade

Skateboard Tough

Slam Dunk

Snowboard Champ

Snowboard Maverick

Snowboard Showdown

Soccer Duel

Soccer Halfback

Soccer Hero

Soccer Scoop

Stealing Home

The Submarine Pitch

The Team That Couldn't Lose

Tight End

Top Wing

Touchdown for Tommy

Tough to Tackle

Wingman on Ice

All available in paperback from Little, Brown and Company

**Previously published as *Baseball Pals*

Matt Christopher®

Sports Bio Bookshelf

Muhammad Ali

Kobe Bryant

Dale Earnhardt Sr.

Jeff Gordon

Tony Hawk

Dwight Howard

LeBron James

Derek Jeter

Michael Jordan

Peyton and Eli Manning

Shaquille O'Neal

Albert Pujols

Jackie Robinson

Alex Rodriguez

Babe Ruth

Tiger Woods